The
Eden Book Society
100 Years of Unseen Horror

A Dedicated Friend

Shirley Longford

First published in 1972
by The Eden Book Society

The Eden Book Society

Copyright © Shirley Longford 1972, 2018
All rights reserved.

The right of Shirley Longford to be identified as the author of this work has been asserted by her in accordance with the Copyright, Designs and Patents Act 1988.

First published in Great Britain in 2018 by The Eden Book Society, an imprint of Cinder House Publishing Limited.

ISBN 9781911585442

Printed and bound in Great Britain by Clays Ltd, Elcograf S.p.A.

www.edenbooksociety.com

www.deadinkbooks.com

About the Society

Established in 1919, The Eden Book Society was a private publisher of horror for nearly 100 years. Presided over by the Eden family, the press passed through the generations publishing short horror novellas to a private list of subscribers. Eden books were always published under pseudonyms and, until now, have never been available to the public.

Dead Ink Books is pleased to announce that it has secured the rights to the entire Eden Book Society backlist and archives. For the first time, these books, nearly a century of unseen British horror, will be available to the public. The original authors are lost to time, but their work remains and we will be faithfully reproducing the publications by reprinting them one year at a time.

We hope that you will join us as we explore the evolving fears of British society as it moved through the 20th century and eventually entered the 21st. We begin our reproduction with 1972, a year of exciting and original horror for the Society.

Shirley Longford

Shirley Longford was born in Derbyshire in 1915. She lived with her grandmother until marrying at the age of 21. Whilst recovering from the birth of her first and only child, she began to write children's books, which were published under a variety of names. Following a car accident, she became estranged from her family and ceased to write for children. Turning to horror, she wrote *A Dedicated Friend* under her grandmother's maiden name. Correspondence willed to The Eden Book Society suggests that she hoped to write romances for Mills & Boon. She may have done so under another identity. She died in Milton Keynes in 1981.

There was a feeling of horror, a kind of bristling in the darkness, and a sense of blood.

– D. H. Lawrence, *Sons and Lovers*

Daisy felt like a fraud, occupying a hospital bed and ordering a hospital meal when there was not a thing wrong with her. But that was what the doctors wanted: she was to stay in hospital overnight so that first thing in the morning they could remove one of her kidneys. It still amazed her that they could take a vital organ out of one person and give it to somebody else, and it would begin to work for them. They had done it with twins in Edinburgh. And they were doing it with all kinds of body parts these days: the liver, the heart, the eyes, or corneas – but in those cases, the donor presumably had to be dead, whereas they would take a kidney while you were still alive. They were still working on the transplantation of lungs; after multiple failed attempts, they were still trying.

Daisy's kidney was to go to her aunt, whose siblings and cousins were either incompatible or insufficiently healthy, whereas Daisy was not only compatible but in perfect health.

'Absolutely perfect,' Dr Dingley had said, going through Daisy's paperwork during her final check prior to admission.

'I've always been very fit and healthy,' said Daisy. 'I've only ever been in hospital to have my tonsils out, and to have my children. I have three children.' She had also had her wisdom teeth out, which technically was a surgical operation.

'And nothing else?' said Dr Dingley.

'Nothing else,' said Daisy. 'And now my kidney, of course.'

'Of course,' said Dr Dingley.

'Nothing else,' said Daisy.

'We need more donors like you, Mrs Howard. I don't suppose you'd let us have your other kidney too?'

Daisy had glanced up at Dr Dingley and opened her mouth but failed to speak.

'I'm only joking,' said Dr Dingley, and then Daisy had relaxed and laughed. 'Although it is true that we don't have enough,' he added. 'We do need more donors, more healthy kidneys.'

A Dedicated Friend

The whole business reminded Daisy of a game that her children had at home, a game in which tweezers were used to remove various items from a dozen or so cavities in the patient. Sometimes these pieces – a broken heart, butterflies in the stomach – could be lifted out cleanly, and sometimes the buzzer went off, and it made such a frightful noise, like an alarm. Some of the parts were missing: the spare ribs, the wish bone. They had perhaps got into the carpet and been hoovered up.

'One's kidney cannot be given to someone who is not a blood relative, of course,' Daisy had said to the doctor. 'Isn't that right? One's kidney cannot be given to a stranger.'

'That will happen,' said Dr Dingley. 'We are making progress all the time.'

※ ※ ※

The worst bit had been the journey to the hospital, the half-hour drive that took her away from her normal life, her home life; she had felt rather tearful, as if something good were coming to an end. But now that she was here, it was easy enough to go along with it all: as soon as she became restless, another nurse or doctor came along needing this or that from her.

On arrival, towards noon, the phlebotomist had taken vials of blood from her. After that, Daisy had been free for a while. She had gone wandering along the main corridor, which was painted yellow and blue, colours that made her think of the beach. There was a chapel and prayer room, where a stranger would listen to her, would speak to her kindly, gently. Daisy had paused outside but had not gone in. She had gone along to the hospital café, and felt almost like a normal citizen, eating a cheese sandwich, drinking a cup of tea, although she kept an eye on the time, mindful of having to go up to the ward. She was just wondering if she had time to stroll outside when her aunt and uncle found her. Uncle Russ was carrying their lunch on a tray, and set it down on Daisy's table before sitting down beside her, while Aunt Camilla sat down on Daisy's other side. In between bites, they talked about their plans for the summer, including a boat holiday with Daisy's parents. Daisy had not made any plans for the summer. 'It will just be nice to get home,' she said.

They went up to the ward together. Daisy's aunt was the first to be given a bed, in a side room. After a little wait, Daisy was given a bed in a bay of four. Two of the beds were next to a window; Daisy's was next to the corridor, but she still had a good view, through the window, of the hospital roofs, flat roofs such as one might escape across in a film.

While Daisy was making herself at home in her corner of the bay, Dr Dingley arrived. He drew the curtains around her bed and had Daisy lie down. After checking

A Dedicated Friend

her abdomen, he marked her skin with a thick black arrow that pointed towards her right kidney. 'If this mark comes off,' he said, 'it will be drawn on again.' He went, once more, through all the risks that were involved in the procedure, after which she had to give her permission for it to go ahead: she signed her name on the line. The curtains were pulled back again and Dr Dingley left.

A nurse arrived with paperwork. Daisy was aware of the three other women in the bay listening as she was questioned.

'Any children?' asked the nurse.

Daisy told her about the girls and Alfie. 'He's only six,' she said.

'Who do you want as your emergency contact?' asked the nurse.

Daisy gave her husband's name, and their home telephone number. 'He's not always there though,' she added.

'Religion?' asked the nurse.

'Methodist,' said Daisy.

The nurse moved her pen down the checklist. 'Do you move your bowels every day?'

When the paperwork was done, Daisy was given a bracelet, a tag to attach to her wrist. She felt thoroughly processed, like lost luggage.

Another nurse came to take the blood pressure, pulse and temperature of each of the women, although one looked as if she was getting ready to leave. 'Are you going home?' asked Daisy. The woman looked at her watch and said, 'Hopefully. I'm just waiting for someone to come and fetch me.'

Wanting to wander, and still relatively free, Daisy went to look for the shop, thinking of buying a snack, perhaps some fruit. Underneath her top was that black arrow, aimed at her right kidney. The shop was halfway down the long corridor, at the end of which was an exit and the car park. It occurred to Daisy, who was still wearing her normal clothes and carrying her handbag, that there was no one to stop her from just walking out.

In the shop, she bought an apple and a banana, and returned to the ward, to her bed. The woman in the corner – well, each of them was in a corner, but the one who had been waiting for someone to fetch her – had gone; her orange squash had disappeared from the windowsill.

And then it was a case of waiting, as if waiting to go somewhere, like when she and Ray had been due to fly out of London Airport for their honeymoon; after hours of delay their flight had been cancelled and they had to stay overnight.

The woman in the opposite bed was named Rita, but everyone called her Peggy. She had come into hospital to have her kidney stones removed but the operation had been cancelled three times now. The first time, Peggy had fasted all night and was waiting to be taken down to the operating theatre when an emergency came in

A Dedicated Friend

and displaced her. On the second occasion, when Peggy had once again fasted and had made it to the operating theatre, a machine broke down and she had to be wheeled back to her bed again. Most recently, it transpired that there was no water in the theatre, no water for washing, so the procedure had to be cancelled. Peggy had been in the hospital for two weeks now and was wondering if it was ever going to happen.

※ ※ ※

Supper was served between five thirty and six o'clock, and Daisy rather liked that, the earliness of it, because then she could imagine that she was, in a way, eating with her children, who would be having their own supper at much the same time. She could imagine their faces as they tucked in, enjoying their food, except for Alfie, the youngest, who did not have his sisters' robust appetite. Daisy's mother-in-law, who was helping out at home while Daisy had the operation, had said to her, 'I'll make him eat.'

The hospital food was soft. It was the sort of food that one could eat even if one had no teeth: soup, shepherd's pie, yoghurt, jelly and ice cream. They no doubt gave it to patients because they were weakened and this food was easy to manage, but Daisy also supposed that eating mashed potato and jelly and ice cream made the patients docile, made them all feel like children, who ought to do as they were told.

Just as she finished her meal and was making her tray tidy, another trolley appeared, with tea and coffee and biscuits. She was reminded of a family seaside holiday in a hotel that brought the desserts to your table on a trolley, and it had been hard to choose, it all looked so tempting – even as you were selecting the Black Forest gateau, you were wondering about the profiteroles and the rum baba.

She was brushing digestive biscuit crumbs from her sheets when she heard what she thought was someone banging nails into something, though lightly, perhaps with one of those smaller, ladylike hammers. The quick, steady rhythm made Daisy think of the Poe story, 'The Tell-Tale Heart', the hideous heart beating beneath the floorboards. Just as Daisy was realising that the hammering sound was not a workman in the distance but someone coming along the corridor, Eliza rounded the corner. She was wearing stiletto heels, going-out shoes, which Daisy thought were rather unsuitable for a hospital.

'Eliza,' she said. 'I wasn't expecting you.'

'I wanted to come and see you,' said Eliza. She stood there, looking down at Daisy, smiling. 'Well,' she said, 'you look the picture of health.'

'The operation's not until tomorrow,' said Daisy.

'Then I'll come again tomorrow,' said Eliza, 'after the operation, and see how you are.' She was wearing a fur stole, which she kept on while she perched on the chair at Daisy's bedside. 'Are you frightened?' she asked.

A Dedicated Friend

'I'm very happy to be doing this,' replied Daisy.

'But are you frightened?' insisted Eliza.

Daisy could have said no. She could have said it brightly, breezily: *No, not a bit!* But she said nothing. She did not want Eliza to know that she was afraid, but she knew that she was a terrible liar and so it would be better if she just kept quiet.

'I would be,' said Eliza, 'if I were you. But it's so much better if you're not; it's no good being frightened when you're going under the knife. Frightened people bleed too much. Did you know that? Fear, anxiety, panic, they push up your blood pressure, so when the surgeon cuts through the blood vessel... Which one are they having?' she asked. 'Which of your kidneys are they taking out? This one? When the surgeon cuts through the blood vessel here, the distended vein bleeds too heavily, and it's very difficult to get such excessive bleeding under control. I expect you've been told how brave you are, going through with this despite the risks to your own health, not to mention the risk of death. Did you understand just what you were getting involved in?'

'The situation has been made quite clear to me,' said Daisy. The transplant team had made sure that she understood the risks; they had gone through them repeatedly: the chance of dying, the chance of organ failure or another life-changing condition, the chance of infection which would make it harder to heal. It became like a litany that she knew by heart. 'The surgeon's very good,' she added.

'You would hope so,' said Eliza. 'One hears all sorts of stories about them, even about the surgeons who are usually very good, perhaps especially the ones who are usually very good. You hear about them doing double shifts, doing private work on the side, working when they're dog-tired or hungover.'

'He's really very good,' said Daisy. 'He's a leading surgeon in his field, a pioneer.'

'Frightened patients also get more infections,' said Eliza. 'They get more complications and find it harder to recover.'

Daisy's hands were lying on her abdomen, above the sheet, and she saw Eliza glance at them, at the right hand twisting the wedding ring around on her left hand.

'You've lost weight,' said Eliza. 'You'd better watch out, or there'll be nothing left of you.' She reached out and placed her hand on top of Daisy's, and Daisy felt the extra weight on her stomach. Their stacked hands suggested the beginning of a game, in which Daisy should now pull out her left hand and lay it on top of Eliza's, and so on, the two of them taking turns to top the pile, their hands slapping down faster and faster, until the whole thing ended in collapse and laughter. She felt the scrape of Eliza's manicured nails against her skin.

A Dedicated Friend

'It is worrying, though, isn't it?' said Eliza. 'Especially at night. That's when all the worries come out. Things like, what if the anaesthetic doesn't work properly? You hear about that happening. You'd be aware of everything. You'd be able to hear them talking – *pass the scalpel*, you know – and you'd be able to feel everything, you'd feel them cutting into you, but you wouldn't be able to speak, you wouldn't be able to open your eyes.'

'I've brought a book with me, to help me settle,' said Daisy, 'but I expect I'll be all right. I've never had any trouble sleeping.'

'Haven't you?' said Eliza. She took her hand away and looked at her watch. 'This is just a flying visit,' she said. 'I have plans tonight. But I did want to see you. Is no one else visiting you? Is Ray not coming to say goodnight?'

'Well,' said Daisy, 'it's hard for Ray because of his work. His mother's at home with the children. Anyway, I'll be out of here soon, if all goes well. Touch wood,' she added, touching the wood-effect laminate surface of her bedside cabinet.

Eliza stood up. 'They've got your name wrong,' she said.

Daisy looked at where the nurse had written her name, and saw that it said 'Daisie'. 'It doesn't matter,' she said.

'Well,' said Eliza, 'I'll be thinking of you. I'm sure everything will work out just as it should.' She leant over the bed to kiss Daisy's cheek. Her painted lips, pressed against Daisy's skin, would leave a mark, a clichéd lipstick kiss such as one might find on the collar of an errant husband's shirt.

Eliza wrapped her stole around her shoulders and walked away. The haze of her fragrance lingered as the clip of her stiletto heels resounded down the long corridor, and Daisy felt like a child kissed goodnight by a mother in evening dress, a mother who smelt of perfume and aperitifs, who was going out for the night.

Daisy reached over to the bedside cabinet and picked up her copy of *Rosemary's Baby*. Ray, seeing her packing it in her hospital bag, had said to her, 'What are you taking that for? You don't want a book like that in the hospital. You don't want to be reading that on your own at night. Take something nice.' But Daisy had not wanted something nice; she had wanted this.

She opened it at the first page and began to read, but when she reached the bottom of the page she found that she had not really taken it in, that she recalled only a handful of words – *groaned... helplessly... stuck...* – and no real meaning. Having reached *anguish*, she had to go back to the start and read through it again, and then again. Reading had always been a comfort to her, but she was finding it hard to concentrate.

The tea trolley came once more before bedtime, and a nurse came round to check the blood pressure, pulse and temperature of each of the women. Daisy got out her wash bag and went down the corridor to use the lavatory

A Dedicated Friend

and brush her teeth. Her gums were receding. They were perfectly healthy: they were pink and tight – the dentist had been very complimentary on that front – but she brushed too hard. She scrubbed and scrubbed at them, and now – *here* and *here*, and *here* – you could see the long root, and how she was rubbing even the root away. If she could not stop, she would get down to the nerves and then she might lose her teeth entirely. It was like a nightmare, to look in the mirror and lift up her top lip and see the long, yellow roots exposed, the gum and the surface of the root scoured away, and by her own hand.

She squeezed out a pea-sized amount of toothpaste, and brushed.

She was back in bed and trying again to concentrate on her book when the ceiling lights went off, first in the bay and then in the corridor, and Daisy took that as a cue. It might be a rule, she thought: lights-out time, like in prison. Daisy abandoned her book and pressed the bedside switch that turned off her own light. Soon, all the lights on the ward were out, with the exception of the nurses' station.

Through the window, she could see the top of a roof, the hard edge of a hospital building, which was darker than the night sky.

༺ ༺ ༺

Shirley Longford

There was a constant hum of background fear, like the hum of electricity that emanated from the pylons near their house, the wires taut between them like the ropes around a boxing ring or like the telegraph wires that carried the phone conversations from house to house; or it was like background radiation, that silent bombardment that came from the sunlight, and from the ground, and from the food that she ate.

They had explained to her about background radiation when they were giving her X-rays. They told her, she thought, so that she would not be afraid, so that she would know that we all lived with radiation every single day, that it was everywhere all the time, and that when they X-rayed her, so that they could look closely at what was inside her, she just got a concentrated dose. But she was afraid. She was afraid of the concentrated dose, and she was afraid of what they might find when they looked inside her.

And there were so many needles. One of the needles that was put into her arm, into the soft skin in the crook of her elbow, had hit a valve. The nurse responsible was very young, perhaps still a student, and not entirely sure what she was doing, thought Daisy, who felt like a guinea pig. She still felt the ache, or thought she did, though perhaps it was just in her mind. She worried about the vein collapsing, or about nerve damage, and having to live with that.

Her sister was a nurse. Daisy imagined that her sister was just wonderful on a ward – competent and kind. She

A Dedicated Friend

had not seen her sister in a while now. She was abroad somewhere.

Daisy had had so much blood drawn in recent months, but still they wanted more. There were so many tests to be done, and there was so much paperwork to be completed. Daisy just let them do what they needed to do, and the nurses were mostly very good. She especially liked one who sounded like Daphne Oxenford on *Listen with Mother*, who said *Are you sitting comfortably?* before beginning a story. And of course there was the matron, who put the fear of God into her staff but she kept them all in line and nothing escaped her and Daisy felt safe in her hands.

❦ ❦ ❦

When, in the subdued bay, she was nearly asleep, a night-shift nurse with a Black Country accent came to Daisy's bedside with a needle, and Daisy had to raise her nightie, revealing the arrow, the arrowhead pointing at unbroken skin as if it had not yet hit its mark. The needle pierced her skin, her belly, and something was injected into her, something that would thin her blood. The nurse left again, and Daisy looked at the clock, whose hands were ticking towards midnight. At midnight, she would be nil by mouth.

Shirley Longford

🙦   🙦   🙦

She woke in the night, hearing voices, the rustle of paperwork, the snapping-shut of ring-binders. She lay quietly for a while and then switched on her lamp, picked up her novel and tried again to begin at the beginning, but a disembodied voice said, 'Put that light out.' It was like being back at school, sleeping in a dormitory with girls who were in charge of you or who bullied you. Daisy complied, switching her light off again. There was still some light coming from the corridor, from the nurses' station, and Daisy tried to hold the book at just the right angle to catch the light, to make out the words on the page, but it was impossible. She gave up, and lay there in the half-light, wondering if Alfie would be all right without her, and if he had remembered to say his prayers.

🙦   🙦   🙦

It was six o'clock. The blinds at the window were open, and must have been open all night. She could see the daylight, the dull white sky. It was still early and might yet brighten up.

On the windowsill, there was a vase of daffodils. They were so perfect that she thought they might be fake.

She was rather hungry but was not allowed to have breakfast. A nurse came to take her blood pressure, pulse

A Dedicated Friend

and temperature. 'Excellent,' said the nurse. She moved on to the other women and another nurse arrived to complete a form, the final check. She said to Daisy, 'Did you do the pregnancy test?'

Daisy looked questioningly at the nurse; no one had mentioned her needing to do one. 'No,' she said.

'They normally do a pregnancy test,' said the nurse, and then, with a wave of her pen, said, 'It doesn't matter.' It was too late now.

The light in the corridor came on again; the hospital was waking up. Before the operation, Daisy was to have a shower. She gathered her things and went along the now bright corridor, hoping to find the shower good and hot.

The water was lukewarm, but it was nice anyway, standing under the shower; she wanted to stay there until it ran cool and then cold, until the tank emptied and the pipes ran dry, until there was no water left in the hospital.

Clean, she returned to her bed. She was perched on the edge when Dr Dingley came into view in the corridor. He was wearing a colourful shirt, such as one might wear on a cruise. He stopped at the nurses' station, and Daisy heard him say to a nurse, 'It's been a long night. I'm tired.' He slipped away then, and Daisy hoped he would manage at least a sit-down and a cup of coffee before he was needed in the operating theatre.

She watched the breakfast trolley come and go, and then the anaesthetist came with a checklist of his own:

caps, crowns, anything that might come loose? He had a Russian accent. It was lovely, the sound of his voice. 'We will put a mask over your face,' he said, 'and you will go to sleep.' He was in his scrubs, and she noticed that the trousers were too short for him, as if they were not really his, as if he were just dressing up. On his feet, he was wearing running shoes – *sneakers* they called them in America, and *bangs* meant a fringe. She came across these American-English words in novels, and had to try to understand their meaning from the context, which was not always easy. Then again, she was not always certain about English terms. The medical staff kept referring to her 'elective' surgery, and Daisy had had to think what that meant: she thought it was something like 'optional', 'not compulsory'.

In the corridor, one of the nurses who had taken her blood pressure was wearing her day clothes. She was going away, to Surrey, she said. How nice that would be, thought Daisy.

Daisy had to remove her watch and her wedding ring, 'and we'll have to take that off you,' said the nurse who was overseeing this, indicating her nail polish, her favourite shade. She had to put on a hospital gown and paper underwear; and she had to put on compression stockings, which made her think of aeroplanes.

From the bed opposite, Peggy said, 'It's not very sexy, is it?'

A Dedicated Friend

'Not very,' agreed Daisy, looking down at her outfit.

They were coming for her now: the nurse with the Daphne Oxenford voice and two big strong men. They took her, on her bed, down to the operating theatre. 'I can walk, though,' said Daisy. It was like a dream, a very strange dream. It seemed wrong to be pushed in her bed like an invalid when she could have walked; it was altogether surreal to find herself prone in a bed, wheeled along the corridors, when she was perfectly well, although rather frightened, as if she were being taken to the guillotine. She thought of Lady Jane Grey, queen for nine days and then accused of treason and beheaded; and she thought of William Wallace, accused of treason and all sorts of atrocities, cut open and eviscerated, cut into pieces to be scattered far and wide.

'There's nothing to worry about, Mrs Howard,' said the nurse. 'You're going to be absolutely fine.'

As before, it was the transition that was the difficult bit: once she was there, she was all right. The nurse spoke to her in soothing tones, and passed her a tissue, like Ray had done at Nana's funeral the month before. There was a series of ante-rooms, in the first of which she had to get off her bed and onto a trolley, leaving her hospital gown open at the back so that they could get at her. They checked her paperwork. 'I need you to sign...' said the anaesthetist, 'ah no, you have already signed it. Is this your signature?' he asked, and she looked and saw that it was. She was taken then to the next ante-room, where they inserted a cannula and attached an intravenous drip, so that now, she thought, she probably did look like somebody who was ill and undergoing urgent treatment, when ironically she was, at this moment, in perfect health.

She recalled Barbara Cartland saying in an interview that women in middle age should avoid being put under general anaesthetic; it would wipe out a quarter of your brain, she had said. Well, it was too late now.

A mask was put over her face and they injected the anaesthetic into the back of her hand, and she felt the coldness of it. 'Deep breaths,' said the anaesthetist.

❧ ❧ ❧

She was lying in a different room, and someone she did not know was sitting beside her, saying, 'That was quick.' There was a clock on the wall of the recovery room, and Daisy saw that some hours had passed. It was rather shocking how suddenly one could slip under, how one could lose all that time. It was strange to think of having been unconscious while someone cut her open and removed a vital organ and stitched her up again; it was strange that such a thing could happen to you without you noticing.

It was her right kidney that they had taken, or had said they would take. She recalled stories about doctors

A Dedicated Friend

removing the wrong organ or amputating a healthy limb, and then presumably it would be necessary for them to go back and remove the other organ, the other limb, the diseased one. She could tell that something had been taken: she ached. It was not really pain though; she understood that would come later. She wondered if she would feel the loss, an imbalance, a lopsidedness.

The nurse at her side said, 'You've been talking a lot of nonsense.'

Daisy was not aware of having said anything, nor of having been awake until now. She wondered what she had been saying, what kind of nonsense, but she did not like to ask. Her throat was parched. She asked for water and her voice sounded small.

The clock had a big, simple face; it made Daisy think of a school room. She recalled learning in a biology lesson that some creatures were able to regrow lost body parts. She had been insufficiently impressed at the time.

She was given a drink of water and a painkiller and was then wheeled, nauseated, back to the ward, back to her bay.

She had various tubes going into and out of her: the intravenous drip, a catheter, a drain, which was draining blood from her abdomen. She was attached by wires to a machine that monitored her blood pressure and her pulse. She was desperate to get better so that she could get home; it was important that she did not get an infection, a temperature, something like that.

When she got home, she would like to go to church. She would like to have a bath and a light breakfast and put on her Sunday best; she would sit through the rather bullying service, on the hard, narrow bench, with a cushion for kneeling on that was too rough through her ten denier stockings or against her bare skin; it was a kind of mortification of the flesh, she thought, although of course there were more extreme examples: there was sackcloth and flagellation; there was fasting and celibacy. When she was little, she thought that mortification had something to do with actual death, as in mortuary and mortician, but it was only a killing of desire, a suppression of the flesh, a cleansing of the soul through corporeal deprivation, through subjection. *Blessed be pain.* A priest had said that. *Sanctified be pain.* She would like to go; it would leave her feeling so much better.

Just now, she hadn't the strength to do anything: taking a sip of water through a straw tired her out; making small-talk with the other women tired her out. If she talked, she might cough or laugh and that hurt her so she tried to avoid it.

'Will your children visit?' asked Peggy, and Daisy had to say that they would not. Ray would not bring the children to the hospital, just as he would not take them to a funeral. He had insisted on keeping them away from

A Dedicated Friend

Nana's funeral. Perhaps that was for the best, but on the other hand it was important to have the opportunity to say goodbye. Alfie did not seem to realise or to be able to remember that Nana had died, and kept asking about her, hoping to see her.

Just as Daisy was thinking that Aunt Camilla would be in the operating theatre now, receiving Daisy's kidney, Uncle Russ came wandering along the corridor, at a loose end. He stopped at Daisy's bedside and asked after Ray. Daisy said that he was sure to be all right, with his mother looking after him. 'Oh yes,' said her uncle. 'If his mother's running the house and cooking his meals he'll hardly notice you're gone.'

'Well,' said Daisy, 'I hope he's missing me a little bit.'

'His mother's an excellent cook,' said her uncle. 'She'll no doubt be teaching those girls of yours as well. You've the two, haven't you?'

'The two girls,' said Daisy, 'and a boy.'

'Oh yes, the boy,' said her uncle. 'Camilla says he's a bit of a drip. A bit of a mummy's boy. I've forgotten his name.'

'No, he's not,' said Daisy. She had a memory then of her aunt saying similar things about her when she was a child: *crybaby*, she had called her, in front of the whole family. 'He's just sensitive,' said Daisy. 'His name's Alfred.'

'Like the king who burnt the cakes,' said her uncle.

How sad that would be, thought Daisy, to live an

almost entirely good life, to be a king and a father, and the one thing everyone remembered about you, what even children knew about you, was that you burnt the cakes; one moment of error, and they might as well have put it on his gravestone to sum him up: *He burnt the cakes.*

The supper trolley came around, with no meal on it for Daisy, who did not want anything anyway.

A nurse came to say that her aunt was back on the ward, back in her room. Daisy, who was not going anywhere just yet, said in her broken voice to Uncle Russ as he left her bedside, 'Give her my love.'

When Daisy tried to move, she felt the ache deep down inside, where her organs were, or were not. She was given a painkiller and a cup of tea. She was not offered biscuits. She still had nausea and drank her tea hoping that it would stay down. They checked the machine, the monitor, regularly, and then less regularly. At half past eight, they found that her temperature was terrifically high, and fetched an electric fan, placing it on her bedside cabinet so that it would blow a constant stream of cold air over her. By half past nine, her temperature was normal again – so that was a short-lived drama, she thought. The electric fan stayed on though.

She did not read; a minute or two of anything was exhausting. She was both refreshed and fatigued by sipping at water or tea. She lay with her eyes closed, hearing the world go by, sinking into a kind of sleep. The interruptions – observations, medication – were brief and quiet. There was something dreamlike about the figures that came to her bedside – first the day shift and then the night shift – measuring this and that and then leaving her again, and in between she drifted and dozed until there they were again, measuring, measuring, as if they were deciding whether or not to buy her and what she might fetch, per pound of flesh.

It grew dark outside: each time she opened her eyes, she saw the night through the open blinds. They came with her bedtime painkillers and with another needle to put into her stomach. Throughout the night, they woke her regularly for observations and then left her to sleep again, and when she woke in the morning, as the striplights came on, she was given more pills. The nurse who was giving them out said, 'How are my ladies this morning?' The response was indistinct, subdued.

Another nurse was closing a window that Daisy had not noticed was open. Looking at the vase of daffodils, which were real after all and worse for wear, the nurse said, 'I think they're almost finished. They're certainly past their best.'

The breakfast trolley came along the corridor and went by without stopping. Daisy had a craving for orange juice – for the vitamins, she thought; she wanted vitamin C, which was good for tissue repair, and for keeping colds at bay. She did not want to get an infection; she wanted to get home. The breakfast trolley returned, though they did not have orange juice. They had cereal, and Daisy opted for Ready Brek. Alfie liked Ready Brek: it was like baby food. The children would have breakfasted already and would be off to school soon.

'How are you feeling?' asked Peggy, who looked dreadfully tired.

Daisy found it hard to think of a reply.

'You were pale,' said Peggy, 'when they brought you back to the ward yesterday.'

'Was I?' said Daisy. The day seemed a blur; it was rather lost to her. She would have to rely on what she was told.

She wondered if Ray might visit. He would be working today of course, but perhaps he would come in the evening, if his mother was taking care of the children's bedtimes.

Someone came to take her blood, a number of vials. Daisy was watching the plunger being drawn back, the blood squirting out of her, when Peggy said, 'Your friend came last night.'

'My friend?' said Daisy.

'The one with the fox fur.'

'Eliza?' said Daisy.

'She came to see you, but you were out for the count. She said to let you know she'd been here.'

Daisy did not like to think of that, of Eliza standing over her, looking down at her while she was sound asleep

A Dedicated Friend

and blissfully unaware. It brought to mind a childhood fear of Santa Claus: the thought of him – so familiar and yet so strange, larger than life and so very powerful – coming into her bedroom, to the side of her bed. He was the man from a song on a Perry Como LP that her mother played each Christmas; the man from 'Santa Claus is Comin' to Town', who saw her when she was sleeping, and knew if she'd been bad, and she had better watch out. She never saw him but she knew that he had been there because he always left her a gift, even if she had been naughty, although it was not always quite what she had wanted, not always quite what she had been expecting, and that, perhaps, she had thought, was because of her transgressions.

When the blood was done, Daisy lay quietly but did not go back to sleep. The corner bed, the one nearest to the daffodils, was missing. Daisy asked Peggy about it, although she realised that she did not know the name of the woman who had that corner. Nodding into the empty corner, she said, 'Do you know where she's gone?' Peggy was not sure. 'She must have gone to have her surgery,' said Daisy, and Peggy agreed: she would be in an operating theatre having something done to her. 'What's she in for?' asked Daisy, but Peggy did not know.

The doctor came into the bay with his team. They stood at the end of Daisy's bed, but spoke to one another rather than to her. They looked at her paperwork;

they frowned down at it, seeming concerned. Finally, the doctor looked at Daisy and advised her to take deep breaths, and to drink enough water, though not too much. 'The first twenty-four, forty-eight hours are critical,' he said, and walked on with his team. As Daisy reached for her water, she thought to herself, *But the first twenty-four hours are already over.*

She ordered a lunch of cheese and tomato pasta and strawberry yoghurt.

'Can you see the trees from where you are?' asked Peggy.

Daisy turned her head to the window even though she already knew that she could not. 'No,' she said, 'not from here.'

She drank more water. She still had the intravenous drip attached as well. All this water, she thought, would leave her feeling as if she'd been rinsed clean; it would leave her feeling nice inside.

The Daphne Oxenford nurse came in and sat down on the edge of Daisy's bed. 'How are you feeling, Mrs Howard?' she asked. *Mrs Howard*, thought Daisy: after all these years of marriage, the name still did not seem to belong to her. It was her mother-in-law's name, not her own. But she was no longer Daisy Middleton either; Daisy Middleton was no more.

Diminished, she wanted to say. *Like damaged goods.* 'All right,' she said. 'How did everything go yesterday?' It seemed odd to have to ask, seeing as she had been there.

A Dedicated Friend

'Oh, it was very quick and easy,' said the nurse. 'And it went so nicely into your aunt.'

'That's good,' said Daisy.

'The next thing we'll do is remove your tubes,' said the nurse, and Daisy thought fleetingly of her Fallopian tubes and her windpipe and that sort of thing, 'and then you'll be able to go and see her.'

Daisy nodded. 'I have hardly any energy,' she said.

'No, you won't have,' said the nurse. 'You'll have no reserves, no backup. You'll feel as if you've hit a brick wall.'

'Yes,' said Daisy.

Lunch arrived. It was not quite what she had ordered – it was a cheese and tomato omelette – but she ate it anyway. She ate terribly slowly; the food went cold on her plate.

After lunch, the nurse arrived with Daisy's medication, painkillers, which did not kill the pain but made it bearable.

As the nurse moved on, the tea trolley appeared. Daisy took some biscuits and put them aside to take home to Alfie.

When the menu came round again, Daisy ordered the cheese and tomato pasta.

Nurses came and removed her tubes – the drip, the catheter, the drain – and she was left feeling wonderfully free, as if she could now skip down the corridor and home, although she could not. They brought her a laxative: they wanted her to open her bowels.

For the first time since the operation, she prepared to leave her bed. When she moved, though, there was pain; when she tried to sit up or twist her torso, there was pain, like a blunt knife hacking at her stomach muscles. She made each movement slowly, gingerly, getting into a sitting position on the edge of her bed, and then getting onto her feet.

She was aware of a desperate, cringing ache in her guts, where something was suddenly missing. She imagined a gap, such as a draft could blow through, although presumably, in fact, her other organs would just shift to fill the space where her kidney had been.

Getting herself from her bed to the lavatory seemed like a Herculean feat. She inched down the corridor, hunchbacked. Seeing that the door to her aunt's room was closed, she went past, glad not to have to stop.

Returning to her own bed was a great relief. She got settled and picked up her book and this time she made it past the first page, and in fact became quite lost in the story and hardly noticed the time passing until she had to go to the lavatory again.

The facilities here – functional, sterile, cold – reminded her of boarding school, and she felt again the same longing for the holidays, that longing to go home.

As she made her way from the lavatory back down the corridor, she saw that the door to her aunt's room was now standing open, and there was her aunt, sitting up in bed,

A Dedicated Friend

saying, 'Here she comes.' It was what she used to say when Daisy was younger and walked into a room full of grown-ups who might have been talking about her, about some bit of mischief that Daisy had got up to, or a bad report card: *Here she comes.*

'How are you feeling?' asked Aunt Camilla.

Uncle Russ, sitting in the visitor's chair, said, 'You look bloody awful.'

'I'm through the worst of it, I hope,' said Daisy. 'How are you?'

'I feel twenty years younger,' said her aunt. 'I felt the benefit instantly.'

'That's good,' said Daisy.

'I'm looking forward to going home.'

'Yes,' said Daisy.

'Has Ray been in?' asked Uncle Russ.

'Not yet,' said Daisy.

Aunt Camilla said to her husband, 'You've hardly left my side, have you?'

'I expect Ray's busy at work or with the children,' said Daisy.

'I thought his mother was helping out,' said her aunt.

'Yes,' said Daisy, 'she is.'

'She's wonderful with children, isn't she?'

'The girls love her.'

'I'm sure Ray will find the time to pop in soon,' said Aunt Camilla. 'In the meantime, you know where we are. Don't go sneaking by, not bothering to come and say hello. We're your family – if your family can't be there for you, who can?'

Daisy lowered herself onto the edge of the bed.

'They don't like you to sit on the bed,' said her aunt.

Daisy, apologising, got to her feet again. She returned to her own bay and was getting carefully into her bed when supper arrived. It was not what she had asked for – it was another cheese and tomato omelette – but she could not manage much of it anyway.

Ray did not come. Exhausted and queasy, Daisy was closing her eyes when she heard the stilettos at the far end of the corridor, coming her way. When Eliza reached her bedside, Daisy said to her, 'There's no need for you to come every day.'

'If I didn't come, you'd be all on your own,' said Eliza.

Daisy pointed out that she was not on her own at all. Peggy was still in her bed, still awaiting her operation.

Eliza looked around the bay, at Peggy, who was sleeping, and at the two unoccupied corners: one bed empty, the other missing altogether. 'You're dropping like flies,' she said.

'That lady,' said Daisy, nodding towards the far corner where the bed was missing, 'will be back soon.' Daisy still did not know the woman's name. 'And I expect Ray will visit at the weekend.'

'I could put the children to bed,' said Eliza.

'Ray's mother will do that,' said Daisy.

A Dedicated Friend

'She's gone home,' said Eliza, and when Daisy gave her a look of astonishment she added, 'I fetched the children from school today, and gave them their tea, and prepared something for Ray. I'd be happy to stay into the evening and put the kids to bed as well, if that's what you'd like, Daisy,' said Eliza. She reached out and patted Daisy's arm, and her fingers had the cold of the outside world on them. 'Here, I brought you something.' She handed over a box of chocolates, soft centres.

'That's very kind of you,' said Daisy. 'You didn't have to bring me anything.'

'They're from Ray,' said Eliza. 'He told me you liked them.'

'I do,' said Daisy. She opened the box and looked for her favourite one, but the space in which it belonged was empty.

'I was tempted,' said Eliza. 'I was bored on the bus, so I helped myself.'

'You're more than welcome,' said Daisy.

'That's very generous of you, Daisy,' said Eliza. 'It can be hard to stop oneself, you know how it is.'

A nurse stopped at Daisy's bedside to do her observations. Wrapping the blood pressure cuff around Daisy's arm, she said to Daisy, 'You've got a very dedicated friend here.'

'We've been friends since school,' said Daisy. She felt the cuff begin to tighten around her arm.

'You were my best friend,' said Eliza. 'My goodness, that seems a long time ago now, doesn't it, Daisy?'

The pressure of the cuff peaked, and there was a moment's discomfort before the cuff deflated again.

'I went to the same university as one of your surgeons,' Eliza said to the nurse. 'Dr Blythe. Our families still ski together.'

'I don't know Dr Blythe,' said Daisy.

'Dr Blythe works with Dr Dingley,' said Eliza.

'Dr Dingley is my consultant,' said Daisy.

'I know,' said Eliza.

'Friends again now though,' said the nurse.

'Our husbands know one another,' said Daisy. 'That's how we met again.'

'Ahh,' said the nurse, as if she were being told a love story with a happy ending.

'And we've been getting to know one another's husbands, haven't we, Daisy?' said Eliza.

'Lovely,' said the nurse, peering at the thermometer.

'I've been looking after Daisy's children,' said Eliza.

'Lovely,' said the nurse again, making a note on Daisy's chart. Daisy imagined a graph, a jagged line like the teeth Alfie drew for tigers and crocodiles, or a straight line.

When the nurse had gone, Daisy turned to Eliza and asked, 'How are the children?'

'The girls are fine,' said Eliza. 'I'm teaching them to sew. They ought at least to know the basics, don't you

A Dedicated Friend

think? If they don't learn how to cook and sew, they'll never keep a husband.'

'A husband?' said Daisy. 'They're only little girls.'

'They're growing up,' said Eliza. 'I had to talk to Anne about the facts of life. She knew nothing.'

'You shouldn't have done that,' said Daisy. 'That's for me to do.'

'She asked me,' said Eliza. 'Anyway, we've all done things that maybe we shouldn't have done, haven't we?'

Daisy looked down at her own hands. They seemed too thin; her wrists and her fingers looked bony. The watch and wedding ring that she had put back on were loose.

The girls liked Eliza, who had once sewn up an inch-long hole that had appeared in Teddy's abdomen. She had narrated the entire procedure, as if she were both anaesthetist and surgeon, while the girls knelt at Eliza's feet, silent, rapt. They still talked about it. 'I can sew just as well,' Daisy had told them. 'I've sewn up many holes in many teddies.' 'But you didn't do it the way Eliza did it,' said the girls. They called Eliza by her first name, as if she were not their mother's friend but their own. The point, of course, was not the sewing; Daisy knew that. It was the *performance* that had won the girls over. Daisy did her mending quietly, while the children were at school, returning the stitched-up bears to their beds and the darned socks to their drawers without a word. Daisy, in fact, had rather hated it, having to watch Eliza turning that little job into a drama; she had found the whole thing rather creepy, and had not liked being forced to be a member of Eliza's audience. She had said so, once, to the girls, but they had not wanted to hear it. 'You didn't have to be there,' they said. Daisy had not spoken about it again, even when the girls did.

'And how's Alfie?' she asked.

'Don't you worry about Alfie,' said Eliza. 'I'm licking him into shape.'

❧   ❧   ❧

In the small hours, Daisy lost the contents of her stomach, the cheese and tomato omelette that she had got down the day before. There seemed to be more coming up than had gone down. She felt ghastly.

Still trying to drink enough water, she had to keep shuffling to the lavatory. Her wretched back would not straighten, so swollen was her belly.

She was on her way back to the bay when she saw the men wheeling Peggy down the corridor in her bed. As they passed, she said, 'Goodbye,' and Peggy said, 'Goodbye.'

Thinking only of getting back to bed, she did not visit her aunt, but her aunt came to her, to say how very well she was feeling. She was holding a bag of sweets and offered one to Daisy, but Daisy could not manage it. 'All the more for us, eh?' said Aunt Camilla to an approaching nurse, who did take one or two.

A Dedicated Friend

※ ※ ※

The nurse delivered Daisy's painkillers; another took blood and observations and, finding that Daisy's blood pressure was low, reattached the intravenous drip. When the doctor did his ward round, he instructed Daisy to drink more water. She was beginning to feel like one of Alfie's old T-shirts, washed until thin and faded.

When the breakfast trolley came, Daisy could not face it. She had been determined to eat well, to regain her strength, but she had no appetite, and she did not think that she could have kept anything down anyway. She did not order lunch either.

The woman from the far corner was brought back onto the ward. They exchanged pleasantries – 'Good morning,' they said – and then they were quiet again.

Daisy lay with her eyes closed, her thoughts roaming. In the afternoon, she decided that she might try to eat something after all. She asked about soup and was given a plate of corned beef and mashed potato that had been left untouched by someone who had been discharged unexpectedly. The food had gone cold but Daisy ate it gratefully and rather quickly. She had barely put down her cutlery when her tray was taken away again.

After lunch, Peggy was wheeled back into the bay. Greeting Daisy and the other woman, she tried to sound cheerful, though she had been reduced to a whisper and looked awfully drained.

A nurse arrived to take a blood pressure reading for each of them. She went around the bay with her cuff, and every one of the readings was low. 'That's all of you,' she said. 'Not one of you has given me a good blood pressure reading.' Each of them gave a little laugh, but they did feel that they had let the nurse down.

※ ※ ※

The days wore on, and Daisy tried to focus on improving enough to be allowed home. She ate her meals and took her pills and rested for hours on end. She wanted so much to see Alfie, and the girls, and Ray. She wondered if Ray would come to see her, if he could find the time; and then, perhaps, when they let her go, he could take her home.

She felt well enough to read her book. She thought in fact that it was quite a therapeutic choice of reading material: she was so glad that she was not Rosemary Woodhouse, whose world was closing in on her, who had no one to turn to.

※ ※ ※

She was just finishing a supper of macaroni cheese followed by jam sponge and custard – which was not the dessert she had ordered but which she ate without complaint – when Eliza arrived.

A Dedicated Friend

'You look quite at home in your hospital bed,' said Eliza, settling herself into the visitor's chair. 'I've brought you something, from Ray.' She put a newspaper down on the bed, on Daisy's tummy.

Seeing that day's date on the newspaper, Daisy said, 'You've seen Ray today then?'

'Of course,' said Eliza. 'I told you, I'm helping out. They're managing just fine without you, by the way. The girls and I made a cake. We ate it at teatime, still warm from the oven.'

'Did Alfie have some?' asked Daisy.

'He didn't want any,' said Eliza, 'but I did insist on him trying it. He's an ungrateful little so-and-so.'

Daisy picked up the newspaper and eyed the headlines.

'Did I tell you,' said Eliza, 'that we've rearranged the furniture?'

'No,' said Daisy, picturing Eliza and her husband Denis spring-cleaning, moving their three piece suite into a more sociable arrangement, moving their kitchen table over so that it would catch the morning sunshine.

'Yes,' said Eliza. 'Ray and I, and the girls, have moved all your furniture.'

'*My* furniture?' asked Daisy.

'Yes,' said Eliza. She described the new layout of the living room, and it seemed to Daisy that their changes would mean having to enter and cross the room at a slightly different angle, otherwise Daisy would be forever bumping her thigh on the arm of the sofa or barking her shin on the coffee table.

'I can always change it back,' said Daisy, 'when I get home.'

'You won't be able to,' said Eliza. 'You're as weak as a kitten. Besides, the girls like the house better the way it is now. Everyone will get used to it soon enough. The hallway tiles have been done too.'

Daisy and Ray had been considering hallway tiles for months, for the best part of a year. The tiles Daisy wanted, Ray did not like; he liked the ones his mother liked, but Daisy found them too pale. They looked, she thought now, like this ward's giant squares of mottled linoleum. She could not imagine them in her own home, in her hallway. Well, if that's what he'd chosen, it was done now.

She turned the newspaper over. 'I can look forward to doing the crossword before bed,' she said, as if she were not already in bed; as if she were at home, in an armchair by the fire, with a glass of brandy on the side table.

The crossword was part of her and Ray's daily routine: Ray started it over breakfast and then Daisy picked at the missing solutions during the course of the day. But when she looked at the puzzle now she saw that it had already been completed. She recognised Ray's handwriting, the clues he had solved, and she recognised Eliza's, whose spiky capital letters filled the remaining squares. 'Oh,' she said. 'You've already done it.'

A Dedicated Friend

'I'm rather good at problem solving,' said Eliza, and, as she stood and gathered her belongings, she added, 'Denis sends his regards.' With her free hand, she reached out and pinched Daisy's cheek, as if Daisy were a child and Eliza were a visiting aunt, or as if Daisy were livestock to be sold at market. 'I swear to God,' she said, 'there'll be nothing left of you soon.'

Then it was the tea trolley, the lavatory, her observations and medication. The pills that she was given in a little paper cup were not the same as she had had before, but she did not notice until the nurse had gone away, and she did not like to call her back just to ask. They must have switched her to a lighter painkiller, or a stronger one. She took the pills with water, and then it was lights-out. The fan remained on, day and night. The breeze, especially when she was falling asleep, made her think of exposed hillsides, the wind in the trees; she pictured the house in *The Wizard of Oz* being torn from its foundations and carried away.

※ ※ ※

Daisy's affair with Eliza's husband had progressed in such a way that by the time Daisy had stopped to think about what she was doing, who would get hurt and what she might lose, she was really too thoroughly embroiled to get out of it very easily; or at least, she had not done so. She had let it go on for too long, until it was too late.

It was hard to pinpoint the moment the affair began. She remembered Denis being with her in the kitchen, after the four of them had been drinking gin in the garden. She was slicing boiled eggs for the children's tea and he had made her laugh, though she could not think now what had been so funny. And there had been the woodland walk on which she and Denis had fallen into step and ended up far from Ray and Eliza. Stumbling over a tree root, Daisy had taken hold of Denis's arm and they had walked along like that until they saw Ray and Eliza in the distance and Denis freed himself. It was months before anything really happened. By then it had come to seem almost inevitable and it would have been terribly difficult to turn back.

The four of them had become regular dinner guests at one another's houses. It was in Eliza's own kitchen – from which Denis was fetching another bottle of wine while Daisy was getting herself a glass of water – that Eliza saw her husband's hand on the small of Daisy's back. It might have looked innocent had it not been for the way Daisy and Denis moved apart when they realised Eliza was there; and the look of horror, of shame, that must have appeared on Daisy's face; and the terrible silence in the room. Eliza would have known then, all of a sudden, just what she had witnessed. Daisy could not begin to imagine how that must have felt.

A Dedicated Friend

As Eliza stood wordlessly between Daisy and the doorway, blocking her exit from the suddenly unbearably warm kitchen, Daisy began to say how sorry she was, to say that they had tried not to, and even before she had finished speaking she thought that perhaps she should have kept quiet, that the situation might still have been recoverable. She wished she could take it back. Instead, she pressed on. It had got out of hand, she heard herself saying. They had tried to stay away from one another. Disentangling themselves had not been easy; it had been painful.

'How hard?' said Eliza. 'How hard did you try?' She told them that she had once seen two dogs on the common; they had been fucking and had got stuck. The dog's swollen prick, she said, was jammed in the bitch's cunt and would not come out. 'That looked rather painful too,' said Eliza. 'Not to mention humiliating. A crowd had gathered; people were looking and laughing at them. The children – there were children there too – were quite shocked, I'm sure you can imagine. Is it possible for a dog to feel humiliated? I expect it is. A bucket of cold water had to be fetched and thrown over the pair of them. That worked.'

'Are you going to tell Ray?' asked Daisy.

But Eliza only said, 'Isn't Daisy the kind of name you give to a cow?' She turned away then and got on with the blanching of vegetables, busy with the meal that she was planning on serving.

Daisy woke early. She felt tired but unable to sleep any more. She tried to think what day it was and decided it was Sunday. Ray would not be able to come to the hospital on a Sunday morning, because of church. He would go with his mother, and afterwards she would make her huge lunch, with which Alfie would struggle. But Daisy hoped to get home anyway, and, if it was at all possible, to get to church herself.

A nurse took Daisy's blood pressure, which was still a little low. When that was done, the phlebotomist came for more vials of blood, though Daisy thought that taking more out would surely not improve her blood pressure.

The day shift arrived, and the breakfast trolley came round. Daisy had bread and butter and jam and tea, much as they had when the dolls had a tea party. It was Alfie who liked a tea party, more so than the girls.

The newspaper that Eliza had brought was still on top of Daisy's bedside cabinet. She picked it up and looked at the first few pages, but it was old news now, and besides, the world to which it related seemed a long way away. She put the newspaper down again.

She looked at the clock. Apart from feeling tired, she felt quite well, and was hopeful that she might be allowed to go home today. When Dr Dingley did his rounds, she

A Dedicated Friend

told him so, and he agreed that she might be able to go home soon, 'perhaps tomorrow,' he said.

'Tomorrow?' said Daisy. 'Not today?'

'Not today,' said Dr Dingley. 'But perhaps tomorrow, or the day after, if you're good.'

'But I'm feeling so much better,' she said.

'You should have a shower today,' said Dr Dingley, moving on.

Still in her hospital gown, Daisy padded slowly along the corridor. She entered the shower room and locked the door behind her. Standing at the sink, she looked in the mirror. She looked like death, or not quite as bad as that but not far off. She removed her hospital gown and studied her reflection. She would not have recognised her body if she had seen it in the street. She looked as if she had lost a fight. Her body was cut and bruised and swollen in unexpected places, alarmingly and asymmetrically. She looked pregnant, but there was nothing in there except gas and bruising, a tender emptiness. It would reduce in size and then go altogether.

When she got out of here, she thought, she would get fit again, get some colour back into her cheeks; she would go running, enjoy some sunshine.

She could hear a fly at the window, the first fly of spring.

She was clean and dry and back in her bed when her parents came into the bay. They had rung the ward and been told that Daisy was not coming out but that they could visit. They found a couple of plastic chairs and brought them to Daisy's bedside.

'It's so nice to see you,' said Daisy, 'although I do wish you could take me with you when you go.'

'But you must do what the doctor says,' said her mother.

They asked how she was doing and she said she was all right.

'It's amazing what you can live without if you have to,' said her father; it was perfectly possible for a person to manage with one kidney, one lung. 'You don't need your gall bladder at all, or your appendix.'

'That's true,' said her mother. 'Someone I know is in hospital right now having her appendix removed. And someone else is having a hysterectomy.'

'I bet you won't even notice it's gone,' said her father. 'They say you can get by with a quarter of a kidney.'

'Maybe that's true, but they're not getting their hands on the other three quarters of this one,' joked Daisy, laying a protective hand over where she guessed her remaining kidney was.

Her parents looked happy and relaxed. Retired now, they had sold the family home and bought a boat and had been sailing around Europe. 'How was the Bay of Biscay?' asked Daisy.

'The Bay of Biscay was lovely,' said her mother. 'We've just come back from the Mediterranean.'

A Dedicated Friend

Daisy worried about them, being at sea in their little boat, and with very little experience. They wrote to her, posting their letters in port towns. By the time these letters reached Daisy, her parents had always moved on; she never really knew where they were. When she said all this, her father said that it was not a little boat: 'It's forty feet long,' he reminded her.

'But that's nothing compared to the size of the sea,' said Daisy. 'How do you manage in bad weather?'

'If you know bad weather is coming, you don't go out in it,' said her father.

'We're fit and strong,' said her mother, 'and we have each other, just as you have Ray to help you through this.'

Uncle Russ was coming into the bay. Overhearing this last comment, he asked, 'Has Ray been in then?'

'No, not yet,' admitted Daisy.

'Hasn't he been in?' asked Daisy's mother in surprise.

'Whyever not?' asked her father.

'I expect he's busy,' said Daisy.

'I expect he is,' said her uncle. 'That friend of yours has made herself available, hasn't she?'

Daisy did not like his tone, but she said, 'Yes, she has.'

'Well then,' said her mother, 'if your friend's got her eye on the children, Ray can come and see you, can't he?'

'It's not just the children though,' said Daisy. 'There's his work, and just now he'll be at church.'

A nurse was approaching, and said to her parents and her uncle, 'We don't allow more than two visitors at a time.'

'I'm so sorry,' said her mother, getting to her feet, along with Daisy's father. 'Well, we still need to visit Camilla,' she said, turning to Russ. 'Shall we do that now?' She bent down and kissed Daisy's forehead, which made Daisy feel like a child in bed with a fever. And then they went, taking their chairs with them, and Uncle Russ went too, the three of them going together down the corridor to Camilla's room – but, supposed Daisy, in a private room with the door closed, no one would see that they were breaking the rules, so no one would stop them.

She read her book for a while, and then lunch arrived, and then the tea trolley, after which she decided to take a walk along the hospital corridor, just for pleasure. Her movements were small and her progress was slow and she was aware that anyone looking at her would see an invalid, but she did feel so much better. Before now, she had always turned left out of the bay, to walk to the lavatory, the shower room, the sluice room; but now she turned right and walked to the other end of the corridor, and came to an emergency exit. Beyond the emergency exit, she could see the fire escape and the rooftops. The door said 'Push bar to open'.

She was fatigued from having walked so far, and was even slower walking back to the bay. When she reached

A Dedicated Friend

her bed and climbed back in, she found that the sheets had been changed in her absence. It was a small comfort; she appreciated it. She closed her eyes and sank into a dreamless doze.

※ ※ ※

'How are you?'

Daisy opened her eyes. She turned her head towards the sound of Ray's voice. There he was, in the bedside chair, holding a bunch of flowers – not a paper-wrapped bouquet from a florist's but a fistful of bluebells.

'Alfie picked them for you,' said Ray, seeing her looking. 'Eliza took him to the bluebell woods.'

'Eliza did?' asked Daisy.

'Yes,' said Ray. 'They walked all the way there and all the way back.'

'But that's miles,' said Daisy. 'He's never walked anything like that with me.'

'Well,' said Ray, 'Eliza wouldn't take no for an answer.'

He put the sagging bluebells down on the bedside cabinet.

'They'll want some water,' said Daisy, and Ray nodded. There was no vase, no appropriate vessel, to hand.

'Eliza said your mother went home,' said Daisy.

'Yes,' said Ray. 'She had Women's Institute business to attend to. Eliza offered to help out instead.'

'I expect she's awfully helpful, isn't she?' said Daisy.

'I don't know what I'd do without her,' said Ray.

'I'll be glad to get home,' said Daisy, 'and take over again.'

'You'll be out of action for weeks yet, though, won't you?' said Ray.

'It will take me some time to get back on my feet,' agreed Daisy, 'but I do want to get home. I want everything to get back to normal.'

'I've already asked Eliza to stay,' said Ray. 'She'll continue to look after the children, and I'm sure she's more than capable of taking care of you as well.'

'That really won't be necessary,' said Daisy.

'We said a prayer for you,' said Ray, 'at church.'

'Did you have lunch at your mother's?' asked Daisy.

'Of course,' said Ray. 'And she appreciated Eliza's help in the kitchen.'

'She doesn't normally like to have anyone else in her kitchen,' said Daisy.

'Eliza's such a good cook though,' said Ray.

'Was Denis there?' asked Daisy.

'No,' said Ray.

❦ ❦ ❦

When Ray had gone, Daisy lay still for a while. She looked at the ceiling tiles: square tiles, like a chess board but with only white squares, as if for a game that would be played by only one side. She turned her head and looked at her

A Dedicated Friend

bunch of wild flowers, lying where they had been left on top of her cabinet, still without water. She would have to ask a nurse to fetch a small vase.

Next to the flowers was the box of chocolates that Eliza had brought in, Ray's gift, for which Daisy now realised she had forgotten to thank him. She lifted off the top tier to look on the bottom layer for the soft centre that she liked, but she found every cavity empty, all the chocolates in the second tray already gone. She thought of Eliza eating them on the bus, on the long journey that she persisted in making. The hospital was not exactly local; Daisy was a long way from home. Or perhaps she had eaten them at Daisy's bedside, whilst watching her sleep.

She put the box away again, and watched a tiny insect crawl out of the bluebells. It crossed the formica surface of the cabinet and disappeared over what must have seemed like a cliff edge to something so small. She wondered what would happen to it; she wondered if it could possibly survive amidst the hospital's mops and cloths, the detergents and disinfectants.

❧   ❧   ❧

She had understood that she might be allowed home this week, but surely the week was now ending and still she was here. Having had a comfortable, unbroken night though, and then finding that her first blood pressure reading of the day was very good, Daisy was optimistic. Having driven Nana home from the hospital more than once, she knew it might still take a few hours: after the doctor's round, the nurses would have to disconnect her drip, take out her cannula, perhaps change the dressings on her wounds, and so on, and the doctor would have to write a discharge letter, and the pharmacist would have to prepare the medication for Daisy to take home, and she would need a lift. She would have to phone Ray, who would not necessarily be there when she called. She could not expect a lift from Eliza, who did not drive, and who, besides, would no doubt be looking after the children. She would not ask her mother-in-law, who had brought her into the hospital but who had gone home now and who had her own life to live. She could not ask her own parents, who were God knows where on their boat, uncontactable. She would not ask Denis, even though she did want to. The last time she saw him, she had said to him, 'Would you drive me to the hospital tomorrow?' but he said he did not think that it would be a good idea.

So she would have to hope that Ray came for her. She did want to get home before Alfie's bedtime, so that she could read him a story and kiss him goodnight.

Either way, she would have some hours to kill, but at least she was getting through her book, although she had started to wonder if Ray had been right about her choice; perhaps she should after all have gone for something less

A Dedicated Friend

harrowing. *Christ,* she thought, turning the page, *this poor woman, lying down in the doctor's fluorescent-lit room, not knowing who she can trust.*

Dr Dingley came into the bay and Daisy said to him, 'May I go home today?'

'Not today,' said Dr Dingley. Observing the expression on Daisy's face, he said, 'Try not to be too disappointed, Mrs Howard. It's important that we do what needs to be done.'

'I am so keen to get home,' said Daisy; 'to be well enough to go home. I wondered about reducing my painkillers, or even coming off them. I might be ready.'

'I don't advise it,' said Dr Dingley.

'But the pain won't get worse now, will it?' asked Daisy.

'It may well,' said Dr Dingley. 'We'll have to see.' He rubbed a hand over his eyes.

'Long hours?' asked Daisy. She remembered what Eliza had said about doctors doing double shifts and extra hours in private practice.

'No rest for the wicked,' said Dr Dingley.

Daisy, who was spending so much time in bed that she had started to worry about her muscles wasting away, said, 'Nothing *but* rest for me.'

'But you've not been wicked, have you, Mrs Howard?' said Dr Dingley, as he turned and walked away.

The bluebells had been moved; they had been put into a vase and placed on the windowsill. One of the curtains that hung between the beds was blocking Daisy's view of them, but if she craned her neck she could just see Alfie's flowers drooping in their vase.

After placing her lunch order, Daisy went to find Aunt Camilla, who was perched on the edge of her bed, eating a bar of chocolate. 'I've got years of a restricted diet to make up for,' said Aunt Camilla. 'I can have whatever I like now.'

'That must be nice,' said Daisy.

Aunt Camilla broke off and ate another square of chocolate. She snapped off a square for Daisy, who did not feel able to eat it. 'Perhaps I could put it aside for Alfie,' she said, but Aunt Camilla said that would be a waste.

'I was hoping to be allowed home,' said Daisy, 'but the doctor says it won't be today.'

'There must be something wrong with you,' said Aunt Camilla. 'They'll have to fix you.' The term brought to mind a cat that needed spaying.

'I don't *feel* like there's anything wrong,' said Daisy.

'But the doctors know what's going on,' said Aunt Camilla. 'They only tell you what they want you to know.'

❧ ❧ ❧

Back in her own bed, Daisy ate her lunch and took her painkillers. She had just picked up her book when a nurse brought in a new woman to occupy the adjacent

A Dedicated Friend

bed. The woman had windblown hair and a rosy glow and was giving the nurse some cheek. Daisy watched as the woman put her belongings into her bedside cabinet and placed a couple of framed photographs on top of it, making a home from home. She turned to Daisy and introduced herself. Daisy did not quite catch the name but did not ask her to repeat it. The woman asked Daisy what she was in for.

'I gave a kidney,' said Daisy.

'That's very generous of you,' said the woman.

'I'm hoping to be allowed home soon,' said Daisy.

The woman turned to smile at Peggy, who had her eyes closed, and at the woman in the far corner, who tried to smile back.

🙞 🙞 🙞

When the evening meal arrived, Daisy began to listen out for Eliza. Sometimes Eliza came while Daisy was still eating, and sometimes she arrived so close to the end of visiting hours that Daisy would think that she wasn't going to come, but then, perhaps even at ten minutes to eight, Daisy would hear the staccato click of stiletto heels coming along the corridor, coming her way. She found herself knowing how many steps it would take for Eliza to reach her, and counting them – *ten, eleven, twelve, thirteen...* – and there she would be, coming into the bay, with her styled hair and her painted nails, with her bright eyes and her vicious heels, coming to Daisy's bedside. Daisy could anticipate her for hours, even when she did not come at all.

She finished her omelette and her sponge pudding, drank a cup of tea and took her pills. She watched the clock.

At ten minutes past eight, Daisy walked slowly down the corridor with her wash bag, still half-expecting to see Eliza before bedtime. She cleansed, toned and moisturised her face and brushed her teeth. She used the lavatory and walked back to the bay. Peggy and the woman in the far corner were sleeping, but the new woman was awake. 'I forgot to bring a book,' said the woman. 'I won't be able to sleep without a book.'

'You can read mine if you like,' said Daisy, walking over to her with *Rosemary's Baby*.

'Have you finished it?' asked the woman.

'Not quite,' said Daisy, 'but I think I'm going to go to sleep.'

The woman took the book and thanked her, and Daisy settled down. Despite the lights being on in the bay and in the corridor, and the light that was still in the sky, sleep came easily.

From time to time during the night she was woken, by nurses with pills and needles, and once by the dazzling beams of a car's headlights shining in through the window, and she thought that Ray might be coming to fetch her

A Dedicated Friend

home. But when, in the morning, she woke in her hospital bed, she realised that she must have been dreaming, that no headlights would shine through the window this high up, and that Ray would not be coming in the middle of the night to fetch her home.

※ ※ ※

When Daisy came back from the lavatory, she thought at first that she had walked into the wrong bay, because Peggy was gone; she had been replaced by another woman. Daisy tried to speak to her, but the woman seemed very confused: she did not know where she was and did not understand what she was doing there.

Daisy was still trying to talk to her when a man came into the bay wanting Daisy. He was young, and wore a doctor's white coat; he had a stethoscope around his neck and carried a clipboard. 'Hello,' he said, 'I'm a doctor.'

Daisy laughed, and it hurt her. *I'm a doctor*. It sounded like a line an actor might deliver – an actor playing a doctor in a comedy – she was thinking of *Carry On Nurse* or *Carry On Doctor*, films in which one thing after another went horrendously wrong. And she thought, too, about something she had read, about an experiment in which a doctor – but a different sort of doctor, a psychologist – had demonstrated that anyone wearing a uniform, such as a doctor's coat, was assumed to have status; they could do pretty much whatever they liked, they could get away with murder.

'I'm Dr White,' he said.

Daisy laughed again. 'You're not,' she said. He held her gaze. She told him, 'That's the name of the doctor in *Happy Families*.' They had a set of the cards and had played the game, but Daisy did not remember finishing it. It had ended rather badly, she thought; the girls had been unkind to Alfie and the game had ended with tears and slammed doors. 'You don't look like him though,' she added. He looked more like the red-faced butcher, though less jolly.

Dr White waited until she had finished talking. He looked down at his clipboard and put it aside. 'I've come to see how everything is, Mrs Howard,' he said, fetching something out of the pocket of his coat.

Daisy had seen so many members of staff here, but she had not seen this doctor before. 'Where's Dr Dingley?' she asked, and his name, when she said it, sounded like something made-up.

'Look up at the ceiling,' said Dr White, as if Daisy might look up and see Dr Dingley there, up on the ceiling, crouched in a corner. He shone his torch into Daisy's eyes. 'Good,' he said. 'I'll be responsible for your care now, Mrs...' He leaned to the side to glance again at the paperwork. 'Mrs Howard.'

A Dedicated Friend

'I had the strangest dream last night,' she said. 'I dreamt I saw car headlights shining in through the window, that window there, and I thought it was my husband coming to fetch me. It was the middle of the night but it all seemed so real. I was so desperate, and I really believed I might be going home.'

'Our minds can convince us of all sorts of things,' said Dr White. He put his stethoscope against her chest to listen to her heart. The focus on her heart led her to think of Denis, and then she wondered if thinking of him would affect her heartbeat; it might cause her heart to skip or race. The doctor would make a note of the abnormality and then he would insist on keeping her in. But he said, without looking at her, 'Good.' He moved the stethoscope to her back. 'Very good,' he said, smiling broadly now at Daisy, seeming pleased with her.

'Will I be allowed home soon?' she asked. 'I was expecting to be out by now. I have young children. I'm keen to get back to them.'

'We're going to keep you in a little longer yet,' said Dr White. 'We want perfect health.'

※ ※ ※

The woman in the adjacent bed – whose name was no doubt written on her board, which Daisy could not see – was changing into her hospital gown. She was not so talkative now. Daisy said again, through the curtains, 'You'll be all right.'

'Are you?' asked the woman. 'Are you all right?'

'I think so,' said Daisy.

'Why aren't they letting you go home then?' asked the woman.

'I don't know,' said Daisy.

The woman went quietly down to the operating theatre, while Daisy ate her breakfast. She thought about finishing her book but of course she had lent it out, and it had not been left where Daisy could see it. She did not want to look in the woman's cabinet, to go through a stranger's things.

In the lull before lunch, she walked down the corridor to Aunt Camilla's room, but there was no one in there. She walked back along the corridor, looking at the floor tiles; she was trying to picture them in her hallway, to see how her home might look now, but she could not.

She walked all the way to the far end of the corridor, for the exercise. From the fire escape door, she could see the entrance to the hospital café, outside which were picnic benches, at one of which Aunt Camilla was sitting with Uncle Russ; she was sitting in the sunshine and drinking coffee, as if she were an ordinary person, an outpatient or even a visitor, free to leave at any time.

Daisy returned to her bay and found that her bedding had been changed. They were so quick, so efficient. They

A Dedicated Friend

sneaked in and out when she was not looking and she never caught them doing it.

※ ※ ※

The woman from the adjacent bed was wheeled back into the bay after lunch. Daisy had been going to ask for her book, but the woman looked so awful, so frightfully pale, that she did not like to. The woman had her eyes closed and kept them closed all afternoon and did not speak.

※ ※ ※

Daisy was coming back from an evening visit to the lavatory when she saw Dr White at the nurses' station. He was talking to a woman. As Daisy drew nearer, she heard her own name, and she heard Dr White saying, '… the remaining kidney being very healthy indeed.' Seeing Daisy, he closed a file that was lying open on the counter top. 'Back to bed, now, Mrs Howard,' he said, taking her arm and returning her to her bed, her clean sheets, smiling only when she was supine again. She felt like a concubine who had only to feed and rest and wait; or like a veal calf that must remain soft.

She lay in bed, expecting Eliza to arrive. She must have drifted off because it was rather late and she was somewhat confused when she suddenly became aware of Eliza's approach; she heard that familiar click of heels on linoleum. She turned her head, but did not see Eliza. She heard voices: the nurse with the Black Country accent was there, and someone else moved into and out of view and Daisy thought that she recognised the woman she had seen with Dr White at the nurses' station. She heard the nurse say 'Dr Blythe'. She did not see the matron, who presumably went home at night; she could not, of course, be there all the time.

A nurse came in to take observations, and Daisy asked if Eliza was there.

'Eliza?' said the nurse.

'Mrs Thundow,' said Daisy. 'My friend.'

'I don't think so,' said the nurse. 'It's bedtime now.'

Dr White came to her bedside and said, 'Are you sleeping?'

'I'm not asleep now,' said Daisy, although she wondered how she could be sure. If the nurse with the needle came and it hurt her then she would know. 'I do sleep, though,' she added. She did not want the doctor to have that to add to her list of problems.

'But not as well as you should,' said Dr White. 'I'm going to give you a pill that will put you to sleep.'

Like their first dog, thought Daisy, which they had told the children had gone to live on a farm. The girls saw through that now, but Alfie still believed it, and still asked about her from time to time.

A Dedicated Friend

Daisy asked Dr White whether he knew if her friend had tried to visit.

'Your friend?' he said. 'When?'

'Just now,' said Daisy.

'I think you've been dreaming again,' he said.

Dr White produced the sleeping pill, turning to the nurse to say, 'Water,' in the same way he might say 'scalpel' or 'forceps' in the middle of surgery. The nurse filled a plastic tumbler from a plastic jug and Daisy took her pill.

'They do say sleep is crucial for healing,' said Daisy. 'They say the body repairs itself while we sleep.'

'They do,' said Dr White.

Daisy settled herself between the starched sheets, her head on her starched pillowcase, and fell asleep so quickly it was like she had laid herself down in a bed of poppies.

※ ※ ※

Even before she opened her eyes, she noticed that the room felt different. For one thing, the fan had been switched off or taken away; its fresh breeze was missing. Instead, there was a strange stillness, total silence.

It took her some effort to get her eyes open, as if she were still half asleep and trying to come out of a dream. And when she did get her eyes open, it took her a moment to understand what she was seeing.

Having gone to bed in one room, in the bay of four, with the woman who was not Peggy sleeping opposite her and the other woman sleeping beside her and Alfie's bluebells on the windowsill, she had woken up in another room, a smaller, private room, with no window at all. There was only artificial light. There was a door, which was closed. She was attached to the bed by various tubes: on one side, a cannula in the back of her hand was attached to an intravenous drip hanging from a metal pole affixed to the head of the bed; and on the other side, she was being monitored by a machine.

She assumed that she must, for some reason, have been moved to a side room like Camilla's, except that it was nothing like Camilla's, which for one thing did have a window. She ought to be grateful, she told herself, to have been given a room of her own. It was just rather lonely. It was nice to see a friendly face, to have someone to whom she could say good morning and goodnight; she would miss that.

She turned her head, looking for a button that would summon a nurse, but there seemed to be nothing like that. While she was looking, the door opened, and Dr White entered, in mid-conversation with a woman whom Daisy did not know. He turned to Daisy. 'Mrs Howard,' he said. 'You'll no doubt be confused.'

'I was when I woke up,' said Daisy. 'I've been moved to a private room, have I?'

A Dedicated Friend

'You have,' said Dr White, 'but a little more than that. You've been moved to a private hospital.'

'Oh!' said Daisy. 'Is anything wrong?'

'Nothing at all,' said Dr White. 'You're doing extremely well. As you'll be aware, we've not felt able to discharge you as yet. We do want to keep a close eye on you, and this is the very best place in which to do so. In addition to the work I do for the hospital in which your procedure took place, I sometimes do some private work at this site. I work with both Dr Dingley and Dr Blythe.' He turned to indicate the woman with whom he had entered. 'Dr Blythe and I made the necessary arrangements during the night.'

'Is that usual?' asked Daisy. 'To transfer a patient at night?'

'A room had become free,' said Dr White. 'One must strike whilst the iron is hot.'

'I didn't wake up,' said Daisy.

'You did not,' said Dr White, smiling down at Daisy. 'The transition was executed without disturbing you in the slightest. I'd given you a sleeping pill, if you recall.'

'So you did,' said Daisy. She turned to the woman. 'And you're Dr Blythe. You know Eliza Thundow, a friend of mine.'

'I know Eliza,' said Dr Blythe. 'I spoke to Eliza quite recently.'

'So she knows I'm here?' asked Daisy.

'She knows you're here,' said Dr Blythe.

'Thank you,' said Daisy. 'And she can let Ray know. What about Aunt Camilla?' Saying 'Aunt Camilla' made her sound like a child. 'Camilla Miller,' she added. Her aunt's full, married name sounded like something from a storybook, a nursery rhyme. 'Does she know I've been moved?'

'Mrs Miller has been discharged,' said Dr Blythe. 'Her husband's taken her home.'

Dr White said to Dr Blythe, 'I'll leave you to it,' and to Daisy he said, 'Please excuse me.'

He left the room and Daisy asked if Dr White would go off duty now. 'He looks terribly tired,' she said.

'Dr White has a few more procedures to perform,' said Dr Blythe.

'Do you know why I'm not allowed to go home yet?' asked Daisy.

'We want to give you a thorough examination, to make a full assessment of your condition,' said Dr Blythe, 'and this is the best place to do so.'

'But is there something wrong with me?' asked Daisy. 'There must be if you're keeping me in.'

'All will become clear in due course,' said Dr Blythe. 'You must be patient.'

'All right,' said Daisy.

'I'll be back in a few minutes,' said Dr Blythe. 'There are nurses just outside,' she added, nodding towards the closed door.

A Dedicated Friend

'I haven't got a call button,' said Daisy. There was nothing on top of the bedside cabinet, inside which she assumed they had put her personal belongings.

'No,' said Dr Blythe. 'Someone will be in to check on you soon.'

Dr Blythe left and Daisy lay waiting until a nurse came in to record her blood pressure, pulse and temperature. When that was done, Daisy, attached to the bed, asked the nurse if she would look in the bedside cabinet for the book she was hoping to finish. The nurse, opening the cabinet door, said, 'There's nothing in there,' and the way in which she had looked – glancing rather than peering, and speaking even as she was glancing – made Daisy think that she'd already known it was empty.

When Dr Blythe returned, she checked Daisy's heart, lungs and eyes, and requested bloodwork to appraise her remaining kidney. The investigation was almost as thorough as the one she'd had before giving her kidney to her aunt, and Daisy said so. 'Of course,' said Dr Blythe. 'That's what you're here for.'

When all the tests were done, Daisy asked about a meal. She did not know what time it was: there was no clock in this room; she did not know what meal she was asking about. In any case, Dr Blythe said, 'There'll be nothing to eat now,' which Daisy took to mean that the kitchen was closed. Dr Blythe instructed the nurse to change Daisy's drip, and while Daisy watched her doing it she realised that she was not really hungry anyway. She could not face another omelette; she might never eat omelettes again.

'I'll have something in the morning,' said Daisy, though the thought of the hospital breakfast trolley hardly stirred her appetite. 'Or when I get home.'

'Perhaps,' said Dr Blythe, and Daisy waited for the rest: *Perhaps I could find you a snack. Perhaps you'll be able to go home tomorrow.* But there was nothing more. The stunted sentence hung between them.

Dr Blythe and the nurse were done with her for now. As they left the room, the nurse dimmed the light and, though Daisy was used to lights-out time, it came as a shock because this time she'd had no warning.

※ ※ ※

She dreamt that she was on her way to the operating theatre. She was in her bed, being wheeled along, with men at either end to do the pushing and pulling, and women on either side to keep an eye on her. 'I can walk, though,' said Daisy, but they ignored her. No one said, 'You're going to be absolutely fine.' No one asked her to sign anything.

※ ※ ※

A Dedicated Friend

'Good morning, Mrs Howard.'

Daisy had woken, but her eyes were still closed. They ached, and she could not open them. She reached for her face, to feel with her fingers. There was some sort of bandage there: padding and bandages weighing down her eyelids, holding them shut. She felt the tug of the cannula in the back of her hand. 'Dr Blythe?' she said, though her voice came out small and it hurt. Someone was at her side, wrapping a cuff around her upper arm. 'What's happened?' whispered Daisy. She felt the cuff inflating like a lung, becoming uncomfortably tight, then deflating again and being removed. 'Is something wrong with my eyes?' Her pulse was taken. 'Is something wrong?' Her temperature was taken.

'Good,' said Dr Blythe, and her voice was further away than Daisy had expected. It was someone else at her side, then – a nurse, who was yawning.

Daisy said again, 'What's happened?' but they did not seem to hear her, even though, when Dr Blythe spoke to the nurse, it was evident that she was now close, that both of them were standing by her bed. They must have been wearing soft shoes, like Alfie's plimsolls, or like the girls' ballet shoes, or the anaesthetist's sneakers, because she could not hear them moving around the room.

Daisy was being raised into a sitting position. She

felt terrible, weak, wounded inside and out. A tumbler of water was put into her hand, and pills, 'for the pain,' said the nurse. Daisy wanted to ask again about her eyes but she wanted the painkillers more. Bringing the water to her lips felt like a game of pin the tail on the donkey in which she was both blindfolded and the donkey. She felt sick, and tired by the effort of lifting and sipping.

Daisy held the tumbler out for the nurse to take away, and in doing so reached or turned in a way that caused her unexpected agony. She put a hand on her abdomen. Through the hospital gown, she felt dressings where she had not had dressings before, wounds where she had not had wounds before. They ran the length and breadth of her torso. She touched the tip of her thumb to the base of her ring finger, feeling the absence of her wedding ring, and understood. They must have operated on her during the night. She imagined the medics bent over her quartered torso, examining her exposed innards, her organs displayed like the contents of a selection box: her kidney, her liver, her lungs, her heart. Her skin prickled as if she were wearing not a cotton gown but a hair shirt.

She heard the door being opened, and closed, and silence.

Join the Society

The Eden Book Society is an ongoing book subscription brought to you by Dead Ink Books. Each book is written by a different author under a pseudonym and each year we select a different year from the society's history to reproduce. There's even a secret newsletter for subscribers only from our resident archivist digging through the Eden family records.

The 1972 books are written by: Andrew Michael Hurley; Alison Moore; Aliya Whiteley; Jenn Ashworth and Richard V. Hirst; Gary Budden; and Sam Mills.

If you would like to subscribe to The Eden Book Society please visit our website.

www.EdenBookSociety.com

The 1972 Subscribers

In 1972 the subscribers to the Eden Book Society were...

Adam Lowe
Adam Rains
Adam Sparshott
Adrienne Ou
Agnes Bookbinder
Aki Schilz
Alan Gregory
Alexandra Dimou
Alice Leuenberger
Alison Moore
Aliya Whiteley
Amanda Faye
Amanda Nixon
Andrew Pattenden
Andy Banks
Andy Haigh
Anna Vaught
Anne Cooper
Anthony Craig Senatore
Ashley Stokes
Audrey Meade
Austin Bowers

Barney Carroll
Becky Lea
Ben Gwalchmai
Ben Nichols
Ben Webster
Benjamin Achrén
Benjamin Myers
Blair Rose
blutac318
Brian Lavelle
C Geoffrey Taylor
C. D. Rose
Catherine Fearns
Catherine Spooner
Cato Vandrare
Chris Adolph and Erika Steiskal
Chris Kerr
Chris Naylor-Ballesteros
Chris Salt
Christopher Ian Smith
Clare Law

Colette
Conor Griffin
Damian Fuller
Dan Coxon
Daniel Ross
Dave Roberts
David Harris
David Hartley
David Hebblethwaite
Debbie Phillips
Dennis Troyer
Derek Devereaux Smith
Edward S Lavery
Elizabeth Nicole Dillon Christjansen
Elizabeth Smith
Eloise Millar
Emily Oram
Eric Damon Walters
Erik Bergstrom
Erin C
Ex Somnia Press
Fat Roland
Françoise Harvey
Gareth E. Rees
Gemma Sharpe
Gia Mancini McCormick

Gina R. Collia
Green Hand Bookshop, Portland, ME
Gregory Martin
Hannah allan
Harry Gallon
Hayley Hart
Heather Askwith
Helen de Búrca
Ian McMillan
Imogen Robertson
Inés G. Labarta
Jack Hook
James Smythe
Jamie Delano
Jamie Lin
Jayne White
Jean Rath
Jen Hinton
Jen Lammey
Jenna H.
Jennifer Bernstein
Jennifer Rainbow
Jim Ryan
Jo Bellamy
John P. Fedele
Jon and Rebecca Cook

Jon Peachey
Joseph Camilleri
Joshua Bartolome
Joshua Cooper
Justine Taylor
Karen Featherstone
Kate Armstrong
Kate Leech
Kathryn Williams
Kelly Hoolihan
Ken Newlands
Kiran Milwood Hargrave
Kirsty Mackay
Laura Carberry
Laura Elliott
Lee Rourke
Livia Llewellyn
Louise Thompson
Lucie McKnight Hardy
Madeleine Anne Pearce
Mairi McKay
Majda Gama
Margot Atwell
Maria Kaffa
Mark Gerrits
Mark John Williamson
Mark Richards

Mark Scholes
Martin van der Grinten
Matt Brandenburg
Matt Neil Hill
Matt Thomas
Matthew Adamson
Matthew Craig
Michael Cieslak
Michael Paley
Mitch Harding
Nancy Johnson
Naomi Booth
Naomi Frisby
Nathan Ballingrud
Nici West
Nick Garrard
Nick Wilson
Nicola Kumar
Nikki Brice
Nina Allan
Owen Clements
Paul Gorman
Paul Hancock
Paul Tremblay
Peter Farr
Peter Haynes
Philip Young

Ray Reigadas
Rhiannon Angharad Grist
Rhodri Viney
Richard Grainger
Richard Kemble
Richard Sheehan
Ricki Schwimmer
Rob Dex
Robb Rauen
Robert P. Goldman
Robin Hargreaves
Robyn Groth
Rodney O'Connor
Rudi Dornemann
Ruth Nassar
S. Kelly
Sanjay Cheriyan Mathew
Sarah R.
Sardonicus
Scarlett Letter
Scarlett Parker
Simon Petherick
Sophie Wright
Spence Fothergill
Stephanie Wasek
Steve Birt
Steven Jasiczek

STORGY Magazine
Taé Tran
Tania
Terra & Bill Jackson
The Contiguous Pashbo
The Paperchain Podcast
Thom Cuell
Thomas Houlton
Tim & Meg
Tim Major
Timothy J. Jarvis
Tom Clarke
Tom Jordan
Tom Ward
Tony Messenger
Tracey Connolly
Tracey Thompson
V Shadow
V. Ganjanakij
Verity Holloway
Vince Haig
Wheeler Pryor
Yvonne Singh
Zoe Mitchell

Also from the Eden Book Society...

Starve Acre
Jonathan Buckley

Everything is buried for a reason. Richard and Juliette Willoughby live in an old farmhouse in North Yorkshire. The place has been called Starve Acre since anyone can remember. Nothing grows there.

There are tales of something interred in the field behind the house. The villagers disagree on what is buried there, but they all know one thing: what was put in the ground should stay in the ground.

Historian Richard decides that he is going to unearth the local mystery for his next book, but he digs up something that only the past can understand. When he brings it into his home, terrible mistakes will have to be relived.

Plunge Hill: A Case Study
J.M. McVulpin

'Dear Maurice, I'm writing to you by candlelight again. Another power cut. I had to carry the papers back and forth in the dark, tiny flames flickering in the stairwells... They've got the petrol generators running in Ward 7 and the noise they make is like a swarm of bees has got into the place...'

In 1972, during the chaotic days of miners' strikes and the three-day week, Bridget 'Brix' Shipley moves to Plunge Hill to start her new job as a medical secretary at the local hospital. As she writes to Maurice, her younger brother, sick at home, it becomes clear that not all is well at Plunge Hill. There are frequent power cuts and she has to work by candlelight. While she'd hoped this might inspire some blitz spirit and solidarity between her, the other secretaries and the medical staff, she's increasingly isolated and seemingly ignored by her co-workers.

Holt House
L. G. Vey

It's a quiet house, sheltered, standing in a mass of tangled old trees called the Holtwood. Raymond watches it. He's been watching it, through a gap in the fence at the bottom of the garden, for weeks. Thinking about the elderly owners, Mr and Mrs Latch, who took him in one night when he was a frightened boy caught up in an emergency. Mr Latch showed him something that was kept in a wardrobe in the spare room. He can't remember what it was. He only knows how sick it made him feel. Raymond watches Holt House. He has to remember what he saw. He has to get inside.

The Castle
Chuck Valentine

Jon's dad was something of a pioneer in 1972, after writing a new kind of book – a book where readers could make their own choices and choose their own way through the story. Unfortunately, the idea was ahead of its time and his father died without ever finding the success he deserved.

It's the summer and, between signing on to the unemployment allowance, Jon's moved back to his hometown to help his mum cope with her grief. Contending with his own grief, he loses himself in his father's unpublished manuscripts. Fiction and reality blend perhaps a little too closely, and when he discovers a hidden appendix he finds that his father's imagination was more terrifying and more powerful than he could have imagined.